The Day It Rained Pink Lemonade

WRITTEN BY: SHAVANTÉ ROYSTER
ILLUSTRATED BY: MONIQUE ROMISCHER

Halo
PUBLISHING
INTERNATIONAL

ISBN: 978-1-61244-927-2
LCCN: 2020921034

Halo Publishing International, LLC
8000 W Interstate 10, Suite 600
San Antonio, Texas 78230
www.halopublishing.com

Printed and bound in the United States of America

To Mom and Dad for being my guiding lights. To Aunt Conchita, who began this journey with me. To Grandma and Grandpa, who gave me a home away from home. This book is dedicated to all the young adventurers out there in the world. May you live a life full of hope and always follow your heart.

Welcome to Jupiter. It is my home. My name is Alto, and I live here with my best friend, Tok.

Early one morning, Tok looked out the window. "Alto! There are pink clouds in the sky!"

I joined him and was surprised by what I saw. Fluffy, pink clouds floated across the sky as far as I could see.

My phone rang so I answered it.

"Hi, Alto!" a friendly voice said. It was Criss, my best friend from Earth.

"Hi, Criss. I'm so happy you called. Something very strange is happening on Jupiter." I told my friend about the pink clouds in the sky. A loud clap of thunder sounded, and I heard the front door close with a bang. I quickly said goodbye to my friend and ran to the door.

Tok stood in the front yard with a cup. It had started to rain, and Tok was filling his cup with rain and drinking it.

"Tok! Stop that at once." I said with a frown on my face. "What are you doing? You shouldn't drink rain."

"It's not rain," Tok said, licking his lips. "It's pink lemonade!"

Tok was right. It didn't look like rain at all. It was pink, and it smelled very sweet.

"Tok, we should go back inside. I don't think you should drink this pink lemonade rain. Please come back in." I begged.

But Tok wouldn't listen. He drank and drank and refilled his cup. Then he drank and drank some more.

12

"My tummy hurts," Tok said.

I took his hand, and we went back inside.

"You had too much, Tok. I think you need to rest."
I gave him a glass of water.

Tok and I stayed up late that night, talking about the
unusual weather. We couldn't figure out what caused
this strange rain. Eventually, we both fell asleep.

When I woke up the next day, it was still raining.
Tok and I stayed inside all day. And the next day.
And the next day too.

I don't know how long it rained, but one day it finally stopped. I ran to the window and could not believe what I saw. All of Jupiter flooded—no houses, nothing but pink lemonade as far as I could see.

"Oh no!" I said. "Wake up, Tok! Come and see!"

Tok blinked his sleepy eyes and came over to the window.

"Yes!" said Tok. "This is wonderful! This is great! Look at all of that pink lemonade!" Then he ran downstairs to the front door.

"Stop!" I shouted. "Don't open the door! The pink lemonade will come in and flood the whole house."

Tok stopped to think for a minute. Then a smile spread across his face.

Tok ran back upstairs into the room. I followed him. But before I could stop him, he opened the window and swam out into the pink lemonade.

I stood by the window and watched him swim away. I didn't know what to do. After a while, when Tok didn't return, I decided to go and look for him. I swam out through the window. I heard singing that sounded far away. I dove down underneath the pink lemonade. I saw Tok and lots of other people and something else I didn't expect.

There was a whole new world underneath the pink lemonade. Everyone was drinking the pink lemonade and singing.

"I am happy and free as I can be under the pink lemonade sea.

There are bubblegum fish that swoosh and swish, filling my heart with glee.

I see rock candy seals and licorice eels happily swimming along.

Lollipop clams skip hand in hand and joyfully sing a song.

I want to be where everything's sweet, and trouble can never find me,

Where I'm happy and free as I can be under the pink lemonade sea."

The world underneath the pink lemonade was beautiful. All the new creatures and all the people there were happy.

Tok saw me and swam over to me with a straw. "Drink!" he said. "Please try the pink lemonade."

I took the straw from Tok and began to sip. The pink lemonade was yummy and sweet, and it made me feel happy. I drank it until I was full. "Do you think Jupiter will stay like this forever?" I asked Tok.

"I don't know, Alto. But I hope so," he said with a smile.

I took Tok's hand and joined the others. Together we drank the pink lemonade rain and sang the pink lemonade song.

CPSIA information can be obtained
at www.ICGtesting.com
Printed in the USA
LVHW070603170321
681674LV00022B/1668